POSITIVELY NO

THE BOOK OF REJECTION

PETER KNIGHT

Cartoons by Ian Dicks

ELM TREE BOOKS · LONDON

TO
MY MOTHER
AND GENEVIEVE

First published in Great Britain 1983
by Elm Tree Books Ltd
Garden House 57-59 Long Acre London WC2E 9JZ

Copyright © 1983 by Peter Knight
Book design by Stafford Cliff

British Library Cataloguing in Publication Data

Knight, Peter
Positively no: the book of rejections.
1. English wit and humor
I. Title
827'.914'08   PN6175

ISBN 0-241-11140-4

Typeset by Pioneer, East Sussex
Printed in Great Britain by Unwin Brothers Limited, The Gresham Press,
Old Woking, Surrey

THE BOOK OF REJECTION

CONTENTS

1

HOW TO WIN AT REJECTION —
AN INTRODUCTION

2

FAMOUS FAILURES

3

EUREKA . . . BUT IT'LL NEVER SELL

4

OH NO! . . . RONEO

5

WHEN YOU KNOW NO MEANS NO

6

. . . BUT I HOPE WE'LL STILL BE FRIENDS

7

THE EDITOR REGRETS . . .

8

A REJECTOR'S RIGHT OF REPLY

9

A FINAL WORD

ACKNOWLEDGEMENTS

Thank you to everyone who helped in the preparation of this book, especially those who risked further refusal by sending me their rejection letters. A special thanks to Peter Bruce, Tony Pinchuck and Genevieve Cooper who encouraged me; and the letter writers who gave me permission to publish their sometimes embarrassing missives.

No thanks at all to those who refused.

Thanks specifically to the David Garnett Estate and the Sophie Partridge Trust for an extract from *Carrington: Letters and Extracts from her Diaries,* ed. David Garnett (Jonathan Cape Ltd); Michael Joseph Ltd for an extract from *The Groucho Letters*; the T. S. Eliot Estate for his unpublished letter to Stewart Deas; the British Broadcasting Corporation for letters on its letterhead; Muriel Segal Colville for her letter to George Bernard Shaw.

Although every effort has been made to ensure that permission for use of all material was obtained, those sources not formally acknowledged here will be included on request in any future editions of this book.

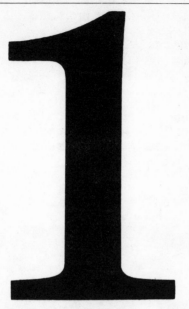

HOW TO WIN AT REJECTION AN INTRODUCTION

'LOOK OUT FOR YOURSELF, OR
THEY'LL PEE ON YOUR GRAVE.'
LOUIS B. MAYER

We've been hiding it for too long. Now it's out of the closet. It's no longer loathsome and embarrassing, rather it's optimistic, hopeful and promising. It's not disaster but opportunity.

And everyone can benefit from a truth known only by a select few: that rejection is a necessary ingredient of success. Winners are those who refuse to be knocked out by a turn-down.

Edmund Hillary's school gym instructor scoffed at his scrawny frame: 'What will they send me next?' he jeered. Sir Edmund became the first man to climb Mt. Everest.

Award-winning novelist V. S. Naipaul was sacked as the Cement and Concrete Association's press officer. They said he couldn't write.

In 1975 Ronald Salle's pop song How Deep is Your Love? *was turned down by every publisher. A few years later he heard the Bee Gees singing it. He sued and won over £3,000,000.*

Composer of three works for coronations, Sir William Walton, failed his final music exam.

Rejection preceded success for Einstein, Puccini, Winston Churchill, George Orwell, Dustin Hoffman, Jack Nicholson and many others . . . including Mrs Thatcher.

10 DOWNING STREET

15th February 1983

Dear Mr. Knight,

On the Prime Minister's behalf I am writing to thank you for your letter of 8th February.

I can confirm that Mrs Thatcher was once turned down for a job by ICI.

I am sorry that I am unable to confirm the second question.

Yours sincerely

Derek Howe

Derek Howe
Political Office

Peter Knight Esq

Rebuffs are quite easy to take because reasons for rejecting are seldom rational or personal.

Sarah got the job instead of you because her daddy's on the board. Deborah doesn't end your relationship in retaliation for you crashing the Morris, but because her hormone level is low and John's got a Porsche.

Your novel wasn't published because they failed to see its significance. You were sacked not for incompetence but for having an affair with the chairman's wife.

Rejections like the above might bring disappointment, but they're too illogical to encourage despair. And even the most boring 'we regret' letters can give grounds for hope, especially when the rejectors display their fallibility by such evidence as:

- Irrationality
- Lack of style
- Want of originality (usually displayed by the overuse of clichés like 'it is with regret').
- Badly typed, misspelt and ungrammatical letters.

Some fail in their attempt to be vicious and others are so kind that you can only be cheered. Discovering rejectors' weaknesses brings the same exhilaration as knocking out the school bully.

REASONS TO FEEL GOOD: DIFFERENT TYPES OF REJECTIONS

1 Semi-Sweet
Using their own lack of success as an excuse to reject can be particularly encouraging, as Sidney Nesham discovered in 1957 when he sent the words of a song to Spike Milligan.

ASSOCIATED LONDON SCRIPTS.

ERIC SYKES.
SPIKE MILLIGAN.
RAY GALTON.
ALAN SIMPSON.

130 UXBRIDGE ROAD,
LONDON, W.12.

SHEpherds Bush 7465.

7th March, 1955.

S. Nesham, Esq.,
69 East Dulwich Road,
London, S. E. 22.

Dear Mr. Nesham,

Thank you for sending me the lyric "Me Old Trumpet" which I don't really think I can use as on the stage I am using a type of comedy which is entirely foreign to this song. It is also entirely foreign to the audience. I am waiting for a foreign audience so I can feel at home.

Yours sincerely,

Spike.

Spike Milligan.

---

2 Sweet

Poet Laureate and church architecture authority, Sir John Betjeman, hates receiving boring letters. So even when rejecting he makes a point of being eloquent and kind. In response to the prolific and persistent Mr. Nesham he wrote:

43, CLOTH FAIR,
LONDON, E.C.I.
September 7th 1966

Dear Mr. Nesham,

Would that I were a variety artist and could make use of your monologues. But I am not. I am an old show-off who mostly makes use of his own work and in the recent series on telly I did some reading from literature of the past.

Yours very truly,

[signature]

And in response to a request for an interview from an Oxford University student publication:

Sir John Betjeman

29, Radnor Walk,
London, SW3 4BP

5th May, 1978.

Dear Mr. Keers,

Yours is a very nice letter and the stained glass in your college Chapel make it my favourite interior, among Oxford chapels. I am afraid I am too heavily committed at the moment to undertake an interview; even this letter has been a bit of an effort *but here comes it*

Yours sincerely,

3 Very Sweet

Every year the BBC receives thousands of unsolicited scripts, anything from one-line gags for Terry Wogan to 13-part situation comedies. They must be exhausted from saying no so often, but you can still rely on the corporation to come up with something almost sickly sweet:

BRITISH BROADCASTING CORPORATION
TELEVISION CENTRE WOOD LANE LONDON W12 7RJ
TELEPHONE 01-743 8000   TELEX: 265781
TELEGRAMS AND CABLES: TELECASTS LONDON TELEX

PK/JSH

15th April, 1992

Dear

"HOW I HUNTED THE LITTLE FELLOWS" by Boris Zhitkov

Keith Williams has asked me to write to you about the above. I am sorry about the delay in replying. We have all now had a chance to look at the book.

And an enchanting book it certainly is: beautifully written and illustrated. I think we all feel that it should remain just that. The television treatment would be unlikely to enhance it.

Nonetheless, thank you for sending it to Plays. I am sending a copy of this letter to Mrs. Bider who has also written to us.

Yours sincerely,

Peter Kosminski,
Special Assistant to
Head of Plays, Drama, Television

4 Semi-Dry

Bob England, manager of the cockney singing duo Chas and Dave, known for their beer adverts and hits like *Bored Stiff* and *There Ain't No Pleasin' You* replied to an aspiring and persistent songwriter:

Towerbell Ltd.

32/4 Gondar Gardens, London, NW6 1HG
telephone 01·794 6702

OUR REF: BE/SE

31 March 1981

John Simons Esq
107 Shrewsbury Avenue
Kenton
Middlesex

Dear John

Thank you very much for your letter of 27th March, and I apologise for the delay in listening to your tape.

However, I have now listened to the songs and unfortunately I was "Bored Stiff" and had to "Turn That Noise Down". I appreciate that there "Aint No Pleasin' You" with this letter but suggest you keep trying in the future, whilst making sure you "Behave Yourself" in the meantime.

I enclose the new Chas and Dave album for your listening pleasure and also your cheek!

Best regards

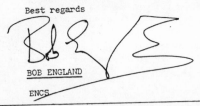

BOB ENGLAND

ENCS

5 Very Dry

Writing to a former student (now wealthy and influential) the Oxford University admission officer said what a pleasure it was to interview his son but felt young Timothy would be happier 'in a larger, or smaller, College'.

George Pitcher, diarist on *Marketing* magazine once applied for a deputy editorship on another journal. The editor replied: 'Considering what the job entails, you must be mad to want it. Since madness is not one of the qualities which I'm looking for in a deputy, I have to turn you down.'

6 Totally Irrational

In 1964 Lord Brabazon was flying out of Heathrow. The airport authorities had named a first class lounge after him so he set off to sit in his own comfort, only to be ejected for reasons he never understood. They demolished the Brabazon Suite shortly afterwards.

Anne Gilhespie was penniless when studying to become a dentist. She had no grant, no income, but many bills. She wrote to her local council asking for a rate rebate. They said:

'Rate rebates are only for people with low *incomes and as you have* no *income at all, you are ineligible to apply.'*

Photographer Elizabeth-Ann Colville submitted slides to a public relations company called Mountain and Molehill who were promoting Woburn Abbey as a tourist attraction. Her photographs were returned with a letter:

'... unfortunately thay (sic) are too authentic to convince the tourists.'

Miss Colville tried taking inauthentic shots but found she wasn't very good at making mountains out of molehills.

A typist applied for a job in Gateshead, Tyne-on-Wear and received a rejection letter with the envelope franked *'Nice to work in Tyne-on-Wear'.*

MP for Newcastle-under-Lyme, John Golding, once worked as a civil service clerk. He was granted leave to study at the London School of Economics and two years later sacked *in absentia* for being over-qualified. The letter ended:

'I am, Sir, your obedient Servant'.

Some professions demand the carrying of unwelcome news. Genealogist Noel Currer-Briggs was commissioned to discover the roots of a grand American woman married to a titled Englishman. She said they were aristocratic and Welsh. He discovered the family was ordinary and came from Bedfordshire.

'Bedfordshire; did you say Bedfordshire? Impossible. A terrible county; all those cabbages. You must be wrong. We are Welsh, I know it. Besides, mother sang beautifully.'

7 What, me incompetent?

When you're being rejected for your supposed incompetence it feels much better when the letter writers inadvertently expose their own deficiencies.

Like this editor who's obviously a man who cares little about public image, Tipp-Ex or the necessity to hit the typewriter space bar occasionally:

FARNHAM CASTLE NEWSPAPERS
LIMITED

Farnham Herald   Haslemere Herald
Alton Herald   Bordon Herald

REG. NO. 798870 ENGLAND

ESTABLISHED 1892

HEAD OFFICE

114/115 WEST STREET
FARNHAM SURREY GU9 7HL

TELEPHONE 22331

Our. Ref   July 13, 1978

From the Editor

Mr Peter Knight
c/o Greenpeace Ltd
47 Whitehall
London

DearMr Knight

        Thank you for applying forthe post of reporter on the Farnham Herald, but I do not think your qualifications fit the bill as far as we are concerned.

        I should hope that with your background you cou d obtain a position more fitting to what you have to offer; not small time local newspaper reporting which is rather a specialised job

        I hope you meet with success

               yours sincerely

               R FHatt

Poetry isn't Roy Castle's speciality. But it doesn't deter the entertainer from rejecting in verse; the quality of which he himself would probably never accept.

A.B.C.
Blackpool.
Aug 18.

Dear Mr Nesham.

Here's the M/s you requested
            last week.

I'm sure that you think I've
            got some kind of cheek

I hope you'll forgive me for
            being a twit

Commitments have made writing
            time hard to git.

Yours — Roy Castle.

Like Mr. Castle, an editor at Dent publishers was tired of sending manuscripts back with the same old boring rejections. One day he received a pile of limericks with a covering letter which read:

> *Limericks have lasting appeal,*
> *So I write to enquire if you feel*
> *You could publish a few*
> *With advantage to you,*
> *While cutting me in on the deal.*

The editor took his chance in one (shaky) hand and instead of saying 'no' in a single uninspiring line, he rhymed it in five:

> *There was a young lady who sent*
> *A book of the limerick to Dent.*
> *Said the ed. I can tell*
> *Such refined verse won't sell*
> *So back to the lady it went.*

8 Scribbles of Nay

People in public life often accuse those on whose whim their celebrity status rests, of making too many demands. True, they have to answer streams of ridiculous questions ranging from the colour of their loo to the power of their magi-mix.

But can there be any excuse for them to scribble on their public's letters by way of reply? The best appear to indulge in this form of vandalism. Like Arthur Marshall:

Hamish Hamilton Limited
Incorporating Hamish Hamilton Children's Books
and Elm Tree Books

Garden House
57-59 Long Acre
London WC2E 9JZ
Telephone 01-836 7733
Telegrams Hamisham, Westcent, London
Cables Hamisham, London WC2
Telex 298265

1st September,1982.

Arthur Marshall Esq.
c/o The BBC
Broadcasting House
London W1A 1AA

Dear Arthur Marshall,

I'm writing to ask for your help.

I'm compiling a humorous book on the subject of rejection. It will include a selection of funny, badly written, cruel, over-kind and generally eccentric rejection letters. One chapter will deal specifically with well known personalities who have been successful in the face of initial rejection.

If you have ever received a rejection letter which made you laugh, curse or cry, I would dearly like to see it. If no letter exists, the story will be equally appreciated. If you've been fortunate enough to avoid rejection, I would appreciate any leads you could give me to help in my research. Your contributions will be acknowledged and no material will be published without your written approval.

I realise that someone in your position has to deal with many similar (but maybe not as daft) requests. But as this is my first book, I desperately need your help to make it a success.

I've enclosed a self-addressed envelope for your reply. It needs no stamp if posted in the UK.

I look forward to hearing from you.

Yours sincerely,

P. Knight

Peter Knight

*Oh dear! I get one of these
every week & just cannot
cope with them. Very sorry.*

Arthur Marshall

Maybe Bernard Shaw was under the same pressure:

November 17th 1941.

Bernard Shaw Esq.
~~Whitehall Court~~   Ayot St Lawrence
~~S. W.~~   Nr Welwyn
                            Herts.

Dear Mr. Shaw,

    Would you be so very kind as to allow us to take a photograph of yourself for publication in "ILLUSTRATED", Odhams Press and in "LIFE", U.S.A. We want to have a photograph of you with the Roosevel-Churchill mugs (~~this is purely editorial and has no advertising~~ tie-up whatsoever and our firm has no concern in any except editorial capacity).

    The idea of a picture of yourself holding a Churchill and a Roosevelt mug in each hand would be a subtle and impressive way of expressing the American and British cooperation.

    Our photographer, Mr. Zoltan Glass, whose work appears regularly in "PICTURE POST", "LIFE" etc. would only require a few moments of your very valuable time and I am sure you will be satisfied with his work.

    We should be most grateful to you for your kind permission for Mr. Glass to take the picture at any time convenient for you and thank you in anticipation.

    Yours faithfully,

    Muriel Segal.

For the BLACK STAR PUBLISHING COMPANY LTD.

No, Muriel. NO.
G. Bernard Shaw
21st Nov. 1941

There can be little reason to take the above turn-downs seriously. Because we're all pretty hopeless at most things, even our rebuffs aren't effective. Instead they encourage creative action and are essentially positive.

The following chapters reveal further inspiring mysteries of rejection, and provide more fuel for our arduous journeys towards success.

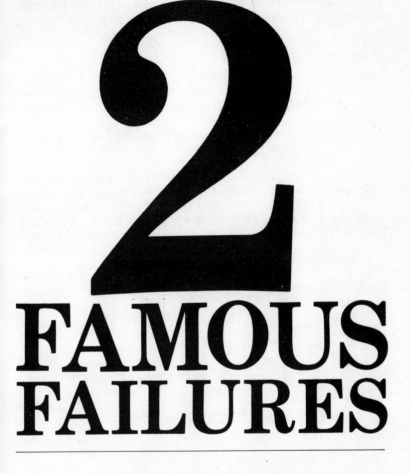

CHAPTER

2

FAMOUS FAILURES

'WHAT COUNTS IS
NOT NECESSARILY THE SIZE OF
THE DOG IN THE FIGHT, IT'S THE
SIZE OF FIGHT IN THE DOG.'
DWIGHT D. EISENHOWER

Fame doesn't necessarily bring happiness, but it must be extremely pleasant. It's also the most effective way of giving the fingers-up to your rejectors — all those aunts, teachers and depressing dissuaders who said you'd never make it.

Acting

Imagine the exhilaration Jack Nicholson felt as he stepped up to accept his Oscar in 1976. Instead of telling his dog, America and the world how much he loved them, he said:

'Most of all I'd like to thank my agent of ten years ago who told me I'd never be an actor.'

Nicholson and Mrs Worthington's daughter weren't the only people advised against going on the stage. Metro Goldwyn Mayer laughed at Fred Astaire during his first audition: 'Balding, skinny, can dance a little,' was their now well known rebuff. Clark Gable twice failed his initial screen tests because Jack Warner thought he behaved like a 'big ape'.

The unemployed Scots actor who, with his burly frame and tattoos looked more like a bouncer than a star, didn't have it any easier. Eager for publicity, his agent took him to meet an influential Fleet Street show-business columnist who dismissed them:

'With a heavy Scottish accent like yours, and an Irish surname like Connery, you're not going to make it, Sean.'

With his short legs and unconventional looks Dustin Hoffman's film career was set for a meteoric fall. But he persisted and eventually won the lead role in *The Graduate* which confirmed his talent and destroyed his critics.

Sophia Loren's physique was more conducive to stardom, but she too had to overcome odds, and it was her willingness to be positive which brought the first break. Although speaking no English she auditioned for a part in *Quo Vadis* and, understanding nothing, answered 'Yes' to every question. Director Mervyn Le Roy soon detected her ploy, but gave her a part as a reward for her courage.

After success in the stage version of *My Fair Lady* Julie Andrews expected the starring role in the film. But the producer thought otherwise and she had to wait for the spectacular success of *Mary Poppins* and *The Sound of Music* before taking her revenge.

Star of *Upstairs Downstairs* and more recently CI5 boss in *The Professionals,* Gordon Jackson was one of six schoolboys sent to the BBC radio studios in Glasgow for *Children's Hour* auditions. 'The other five were chosen and I wasn't.'

But with the help of his teacher he auditioned again and succeeded. 'I suppose that's what started me off on my acting career. If it hadn't been for that teacher encouraging me to try again, I'd be in a drawing office in Glasgow, as most Scotsmen then ended up as engineers or draughtsmen.'

Before succeeding in *Take Three Girls*, television actress Angela Down received unsound advice from Peter Hall, now the head of the National Theatre, but formerly director of the Royal Shakespeare Company. After a season of walk-on parts at Stratford he drew her aside and said she might do better in some other occupation.

'Since the only job I could come up with was a florist, I thought I'd better stay with it and hope his would be a minority opinion.'

She went on to a successful TV career and regular work at Peter Hall's National Theatre.

If anyone proves that the greater the rejection the more glorious the success, it's that paragon of actresses, Miss Piggy.

'Moi, rejected? Isn't this subject a teensy weensy bit tasteless? In my case it proves, simplement, *that true beauty and talent always win through'.*

The sex goddess and her colleagues thought they'd never make it really big. They were a parochial success in Washington, a minor attraction on *Sesame Street* and were sometimes invited on to trendy television chat shows. But the American networks didn't think Jim Henson's creations were good enough to go nationwide.

It took Lew Grade to spot the little piglette's talent. With his backing there was global triumph for Kermit, Gonzo and Miss Piggy's fellow Muppets. (Lord Grade's popularity didn't last as long. He was deposed as chief frog at Associated Communications.)

Journalism

While it's easy to plot the rise of such notables as Miss Piggy, others like TV presenter David Frost, as Kitty Muggeridge said, 'rose without trace'. Actually Frost did leave a trail and it included being sacked from his first job as a trainee producer at Rediffusion Television.

Malcolm Muggeridge was one of the first to realise that there were profits to be made out of rejection: 'The only way of making money out of journalism is to be sacked regularly.'

After he lost his job as the *Guardian*'s Moscow correspondent in the '30s, Muggeridge returned to Britain where *The Times* and the BBC (among many others) told him they didn't need his services. In 1933 he wrote: 'There is nothing before me but failure . . . failure eating away like a disease.'

But he overcame his depression, went on to edit *Punch* and became a media sage who in a burst of publicity in 1982 accepted what he had always rejected — Christianity and the Roman Catholic Church.

Jean Rook, known as the 'First Lady of Fleet Street' had a hard introduction to the newsdesk. She writes:

"At my very first interview for a job, the News Editor of the Hull Daily Mail crumpled me into a ball and chucked my hopes of a journalistic career into his waste paper basket.
    "I was 'too old' (25). I should have left school at 14 with 140 w.p.m. Pitman's instead of an M.A. thesis on T.S.Eliot. The only education I lacked, he said, snapping me across like his well-chewed pencil, was LIFE.
    "LIFE involved taking notes on Hull flower shows, mayor makings, local Thespians and Rotary lunches. He himself had been doing LIFE, practically since Creation, and he hinted that I was an over-educated playgirl unworthy to wash the keys of his typewriter.

"No. let's report that verbatim. He did not hint. He actually said, 'Editing London University's newspaper means nothing in real LIFE. I could never offer you a job of such great responsibility as a reporter on the Hull Daily Mail. Forget journalism, because, I can tell you now, you'll never, never get to Fleet Street.'

"As I walked from his office, I knew the first step I took would get me to Fleet Street if I had to arrive on crutches. Or in a bath chair. Weeks later, the Sheffield Telegraph took me on as a graduate trainee.

"So I owe the Hull Daily Mail man a lot. If I could remember his name.

I trust he knows mine."

It was Miss Rook's newspaper, the *Daily Express,* which sacked young reporter Raymond Chandler in the 1920s. Every time they sent him on a story he'd lose his way. After an unsuccessful attempt at freelancing he emigrated to America and there built up the prosperous South Basin Oil Company. But following a drinking binge he was again fired. So at the age of 44 he sat down at his typewriter and created Philip Marlowe, one of the most successful fictional detectives ever.

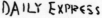

DAILY EXPRESS

British Negativity

The British have a nasty habit of rejecting before they accept. Sir Winston Churchill's master at Harrow saw no future for the boy and Sandhurst military college rejected him twice.

Stanley Matthews, the first English international footballer to be knighted, was dismissed by a sports writer: 'He lacks big match temperament. He'll never hold down a first team place in top class soccer.'

And Jimmy Young, not yet 'Sir' but with a daily following of eight million listeners on Radio 2, was dismissed from his first BBC audition and told he'd never make a radio announcer, let alone produce a successful 'prog'.

G. K. Chesterton, an overweight child, was said by his teacher to be a useless human with no future and only fat in his brain.

Mozart was sacked as court composer after the performance of his first opera, *Idomeneo*. The Royal and Imperial Conservatoire in Milan told Giuseppe Verdi that his mediocrity prevented them from accepting him and Giocomo Puccini's music teacher dismissed him as talentless. His opera, *Madame Butterfly*, was a glorious flop on the opening night.

'If Beethoven's seventh symphony is not by some means abridged, it will soon fall into disuse,' predicted a Boston critic.

In 1956 a young cartoonist called Melville Calman sent some of his work to *Punch.* They returned his offerings (which now appear regularly in the *Times* and *Sunday Times*) with a covering letter distinguished by its total lack of encouragement, humour or foresight.

PUNCH
10 BOUVERIE STREET
LONDON
E.C.4

TELEGRAMS:
CHARIVARI, FLEET, LONDON

TELEPHONE:
FLEET STREET 9161 (6 LINES)

Melville S. Calman, Esq.,
64, Linthorpe Road,
London. N.16.

18th. September,
1956.

Dear Calman,

      I rather doubt if "cartooning" (as it is generally called) is really your line. Neither drawings or ideas measure up to the standard required here, I'm afraid.

      "City/Country" is a closed shop; we have two artists quite good at it and only one can we use.

      Many regrets.

Russell Brockbank

Science

Einstein's parents thought him retarded. The boy failed to get into the Munich Technical Institute and was forced to do the preliminary work on his theory of relativity while working for the post office.

Gregor Mendel, founder of the science of genetics, failed at university. His teachers said he lacked 'the requisite clarity of thought to be a scientist'. And Thomas Edison's teachers predicted failure because of his 'addled state'.

Art

For artists it's almost a cheat to be immediately accepted. Rejection is complimentary . . . for a while. In 1863 the French Impressionists found themselves excluded from the *Salon* and protested so loudly that Napoleon III organised an alternative exhibition called the *Salon des Refuses*. It brought acceptance for Manet, Pissaro, Renoir, Degas and others.

Picasso was luckier than Van Gogh and Rembrandt. He was acclaimed and became wealthy in his own lifetime, but times were hard at first. Trying to hawk his pictures in Paris he was caught in a rain storm outside a chic gallery. He went in and asked for shelter. They threw him and his paintings out.

Politics

In few professions can the risk of personal refusal be higher than in politics. Before prospective MPs can attempt to win votes from strangers, they have to convince their own kind during the local selection process. This is when many aspirant parliamentarians discover that grass roots can pack a powerful kick.

Veteran Tory MP for Brighton, Julian Amery, recalls his failed efforts to gain a seat: 'Someone [on the selection committee] asked if I was married or engaged. I admitted that I was still a bachelor but at twenty-one there was still time to correct this defect. Why, I might even find my soul mate in the confines of the constituency. This went down rather well.

'Nevertheless a few days later I heard from the chairman that his committee had decided against me, because they felt they really must have a married man ... The man selected instead of me turned out to be a bigamist.'

Liberal leader David Steel auditioned in 1964 as a presenter on Scottish Television. He failed. But after he became an MP they gave him a job presenting a weekly Sunday evening programme, proving it's not what you know, but who ...

'I was rejected for a parliamentary seat,' says Bath MP Chris Patten, 'on the grounds that I didn't have a sense of humour. That sort of thing is no laughing matter.'

His boss, Mrs Margaret Thatcher, after being turned down by ICI, was determined to become an MP. When she applied to Beckenham and later Maidstone she had already acquired a husband and twins. Both constituencies rejected her saying she'd do better to stay at home and look after her babies.

3

EUREKA
BUT IT'LL NEVER SELL

'I CAN ANSWER YOU IN
TWO WORDS: IM POSSIBLE.'
SAM GOLDWYN

British Rail have plans for intergalactic travel. They've invented a nuclear-powered flying saucer which could whisk you from Victoria to Venus in the time it takes Jimmy Savile to light a cigar.

This development might come as some surprise to travellers who in 1982 tested BR's other spectacular invention, the Advanced Passenger Train (APT). Using a revolutionary tilting device the APT was, unlike any other train, supposed to take corners at speeds of 160 miles per hour. It did, but tended to remain tilted on the straight bits too and was quietly shunted into a disused siding.

So sceptics might be justified in thinking BR has ideas above its station. But they're being as narrow minded as Dr. Dionysus Lardner, a nineteenth century professor of astronomy at London University who jeered at the very idea of high speed rail travel because he predicted passengers would die of asphyxia. Poor Dr. Lardner — but he was only conforming to the universal tendency to reject new ideas. We've turned down virtually every innovation from rockets to roll-on deodorant.

Flying — utterly impossible

'Flight by machines heavier than air is unpractical and insignificant if not utterly impossible,' said astronomer Simon Newcomb in 1901. Eighteen months later Orville and Wilbur Wright flew and Professor Newcomb ate whatever astronomers eat if they don't wear hats. But his embarrassment wasn't enough to prevent further foolish statements about the development of flight.

Rockets — ridiculous

Unknown to each other, two pioneers were having an equally unsuccessful time on opposite sides of the world trying to convince their peers that rocket propulsion was a serious concept.

In 1923 a Transylvanian student, Hermann Oberth, published a book called *The Rocket into Interplanetary Space* which was a big miss with the scientists. Meanwhile Dr. Robert Goddard had moved in with his aunt on her farm in Massachusetts and was disturbing distant neighbours with tremendous wooshes and bangs. So much so that they nearly stopped him experimenting with the liquid rocket propellants which would many years later thrust monkeys, dogs and people into space.

It was Dr. Robert Goddard too, who in 1902 proudly wrote off to the scientific journal *Popular Astronomy* about his theory for nuclear power. He received a curt reply from its editor:

'The speculation . . . is interesting, but the impossibility of ever doing it is so certain that it is not practically possible.'

Goddard ignored both the editor and his irritable neighbours. Meanwhile in Germany, work was slowly progressing on the rocket which would eventually propel the destructive buzz bomb — one of the world's first effective long-range missiles.

Fortunately for Britain, Hitler woke up in a sceptical mood one morning after dreaming that no rocket would ever reach England, and stopped most of the research funds. The British Government once shared similar pessimism. In 1933 an Undersecretary of State wrote to the chairman of the British Interplanetary Society:

"We follow with interest any work being done in other countries on jet propulsion, but scientific investigation into the possibilities has given no indication that this method can be a serious competitor to the airscrew engine combination. We do not consider we should be justified in spending any time or money on it ourselves."

Lasers — a switch off

We use the energy from concentrated rays of light for a variety of tasks from curing cancer to creating intriguing disco light shows. But as recently as 1960 the idea was laughable. Theodore Mainman sent particulars of his helium-neon laser to the respected journal *Physical Review Letters* in June 1960. They sent them back.

Jets — but what about the propeller?

Official penchant for positivity saw to it that Britain fought most of the Second World War with piston engines instead of the superior jet fighters. In the 1920s A. A. Griffith, a lowly government research scientist, designed a gas turbine to drive a propeller. His superiors didn't think much of his invention. He had just built the prototype when they transferred him to Air Ministry laboratories in South Kensington where facilities were totally inadequate. Mr. Griffith gave up.

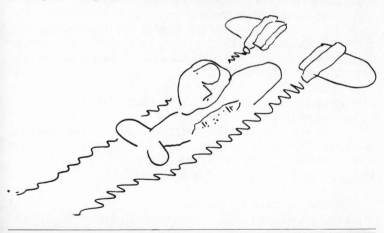

At about the same time Frank Whittle, an RAF scientist, was designing the jet engine which he patented in 1929. Whitehall thought it was a bit of a joke and so did the aero industry. The RAF decided that their employee needed educating and sent Whittle to Cambridge to study Mechanical Science.

Discouraged, he let the patent lapse in 1935. But his conviction of the jet's viability was strong enough to overcome his dejection and he finally managed to get limited support from City bankers. Development work continued slowly. Whittle pleaded for time off and in a fit of generosity the Air Ministry allowed him to work on the project for a meagre six hours a week.

Their attitude changed fast when war broke out in 1939. The Gloster-Whittle jet flew two years later, but because of the long development time needed, official scepticism saw to it that the 'plane made no significant impact on the war.

Meanwhile keen interest from German industrialists meant that the Nazi jet was advancing fast. Fortunately for the British, Nazi officials were as insecure about dispensing with their precious pistons and propellers. The German Air Ministry refused to take scientists' claims seriously and no jet fighters were ordered in time to pose a threat to the RAF.

VW Beetle — not worth a damn

After the Second World War the British proved that emulating Nelson by raising the eye-glass to the blind eye can mean missing the main chance.

While evaluating German assets for reparations the British and American delegation had a look around the Volkswagen factory which produced Hitler's slow revving 'people's car', the Beetle.

Granted it was a funny looking thing that made a strange putting noise, but Sir William Rootes's reaction to what was to become the biggest selling car in the world was a bit over the top. He said: 'The Volkswagen does not meet the fundamental technical requirements of a motor car.' Ernest Breech, president of Ford, who was also on the trip, said it was 'not worth a damn'.

Telephones — toys for the boys

Alexander Graham Bell, a Scotsman living in the United

States, didn't have an easy time selling his canny invention. He developed the telephone while teaching deaf children, but received little encouragement from investors. One, J. Murray Forbes, an eminent Bostonian, thought of investing but after a visit to Bell's laboratories concluded that the sound didn't travel through wire. Someone, he said, sat on the roof shouting down 'some kind of horn'.

Even when the invention proved itself there were few takers. Tired of the struggle Bell offered all rights to the great American telegraph company, Western Union. Their president, William Orton, scoffed at the deal: 'What use could this company make of an electrical toy?'

Talkies — it'll never catch on
Auguste Lumière, inventor of film's forerunner, the peepshow, refused to believe in the value of his machine:

'It can be exploited for a certain time as a scientific curiosity, but apart from that it has no commercial value whatsoever.'

Although Lumière was proved wrong, his successors who should have known better were equally negative. In 1924 the director of great silent epics, D. W. Griffith, predicted that there wouldn't ever be talk on film.

'It will never be possible to synchronise the voice with the pictures.'

And H. B. Warner of Warner Brothers was as sceptical:

'Who the hell wants to hear actors talk?'

Television — no one's got the time to watch
In 1939, when talkies were well established but television, invented by John Logie Baird, was only starting up, the *New York Times* made a prediction:

> "The problem with television is that the people must sit and keep their eyes glued to a screen; the average American family hasn't time for it. Therefore the showmen are convinced that for this reason, if no other, television will never be a serious competitor of broadcasting.

Typewriters — simply a mechanical curiosity
Invented in 1714 by Henry Mills, it wasn't until the late nineteenth century that the typewriter was accepted. In

1897, twenty-three years after Mark Twain had proved the machine's usefulness by typing the manuscript of *Life on the Mississippi*, the Remington Arms Company was offered the rights to a typewriter. They decided that 'no mere machine can replace a reliable and honest clerk.'

The same machine was later bought by the Underwood Company who sold 12,000,000 of what Mark Twain called 'a curiosity breeding little joker.'

Ball points — disbelieving the brothers Biro

It wasn't until the 1940s that one of the greatest clerical revolutions took place. At last white collar workers had something easier to pilfer than loo rolls. The Biro had been born.

It could have been earlier if John Loud's 1888 invention for writing on rough surfaces — a rudimentary ball point — had been accepted. It had to wait until the brothers Biro, George and Ladislao, moved from Hungary to Buenos Aires and there made the first nibless pens.

Their invention was finally offered to the world by Eversharp in 1946. The French company, BiC, now sell more than 12,000,000 ballpoints a day.

Photocopy — zany xerographer

Another office wonder — the photocopier — took even longer to reach reality. Patent lawyer, Chester Carlson, decided that the only way to get rich was to invent something. In 1937 he filed a patent for the Xerography process but it took him twenty-three years of concerted effort before he saw the first commercial photocopier, and his money.

Rayon — give them the real thing

Samuel Courtauld didn't have to wait that long for his invention — rayon — to pay. But he had to fight equally hard. Shortly after he discovered synthetic silk he proudly went to sell the process to one of the country's most prosperous silk mills, Listers & Co. of Bradford. They sent him straight to his fortune by rejecting the offer, saying the public wanted the real thing. Sam Courtauld manufactured rayon himself and proved otherwise.

Zip — but buttons don't burst

The rag trade showed an equal lack of interest in Whitcomb L. Judson's cranky invention — the zip. It took thirty years for it to be taken seriously and had to be sold door to door because clothes manufacturers were worried about embarrassing bursts.

Safety razor — a cut-throat business

The cut and thrust of King Camp Gillette and his innovation — the safety razor — caused gasps of boredom, mainly from metallurgists who said it was impossible to produce a thin, pliable and sharp blade. Gillette refused to believe them and finally produced his razor.

The determination shown by Messrs Whittle, Gillette *et al* is perhaps more inspirational than the inventions which have enabled us, among other things, to fly fast in zipped clothes with smooth cheeks.

Not content with designing a society which relies on the acceptance of a few and rejection of many, man (and this is one area from which women should be glad to be excluded) has now extended the possibilities of the irrational rebuff. He has created machines which make decisions that affect us in a number of ways, mostly embarrassing. The credit card computer that disowns us as we're trying to pay a huge restaurant bill; the railway station vending machine which takes our money and then stubbornly (and in full view of other dieting travellers) refuses to give us the chocolate; the automatic door that closes in our face; the cash dispenser which takes away our card and leaves us penniless even though we have hundreds of pounds in the bank.

A respected *Financial Times* journalist sold his car in Newmarket on a Saturday. With a large cheque in his pocket and his new girlfriend by his side he headed for the nearest cash dispenser, needing money for the train fare home. It accepted his card eagerly. After various humming noises the protective window snapped shut and a message flashed on to the screen: 'You are overdrawn. Your card is being retained. Contact your branch.'

Brian Dagnall of Portsmouth wrote to a mailing company asking to be removed from their list but they said it was impossible. Their computer, they explained, was the only thing which knew Mr. Dagnall's code number and without it no de-programming could take place. He was told to wait until the next mail arrived and then return the envelopes. The computer would see what it could do.

One Saturday Kathleen Stubbs of Stoke-on-Trent put her clothes into a self-service dry cleaning machine, pumped in the money and waited for a half-hour wash. After an hour she tried and failed to stop the tumbling.

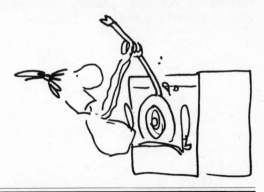

After two hours she called the police. They called the fire brigade. Four hours later they stopped the machine but couldn't open it. Two days later Kathleen's clothes were returned, very clean.

Phoning the Legal Technology Control Group can be frustrating. An automatic voice often says: 'The lines are being used by our computer, so you've been connected to an answering machine.'

There is a close resemblance between these 'systems' and civil servants. They possess the same remoteness and inflexibility, but it is their rank stupidity which really riles; their blatantly impersonal touch which sparks our sense of justice, or more appropriately, our spirit of revenge.

In an attempt to increase their public revenue the new Zimbabwean government sent income tax forms to a number of people who had never paid tax before. From one potential contributor came the following reply: 'I have to refer to the attached form. I regret so grave I am unable to complete the form, as I do not know what is meant by filling this form. However, I am not interested in this income service. Could you please cancel my name in your books, as this system has upset my mind and I do not know who registered me as one of your customers.'

Occasionally, replies can be explosive . . . as some Swedish businessmen discovered at the turn of the century. An inventor posted his latest invention to all the executives who had callously rejected his previous ideas. They received the first letter bombs.

4

OH NO! RONEO

'THE WORST SIN TOWARDS OUR FELLOW CREATURES IS NOT TO HATE THEM, BUT TO BE INDIFFERENT TO THEM; THAT'S THE ESSENCE OF INHUMANITY.'
G. BERNARD SHAW

It's different from the gas bill, telephone account and the latest *Reader's Digest* lucky numbers. It's not filled with double glazing special offers and it doesn't make the same plop as it hits the floor. But it's as recognisable.

One way of identifying a job rejection letter is by the manner in which it falls. Because of its lightness it hits ground later than the rest of the mail, sometimes gliding a little on the way down. So you'll seldom find one directly below the letter flap; they prefer to scoot away and sheepishly cling to the skirting board.

There are also two other clues: type of envelope and postage cost. The cheapest envelope, preferred by those who reject in bulk, is the brown manilla. If it arrives with a second class stamp (bad news in this business travels cheap and slow) you can safely assume that, for some totally irrational reason, the job's gone to someone else.

Once the letter's opened, the 'we regrets', 'on files' and similar recruitment clichés glow like distress flares on a sea of negativity; and confirm any doubts you might have had about the contents. It can be an unpleasant read, but even in these unshared moments of disappointment there's pleasure to be found in the detection of trends, styles and excuses.

TRENDS
Recruitment rejections fall into four main groups:

- The Two-Tone
- The Word-Processed
- The Impersonal Insult
- The Poverty Trap

The Two-Tone
It's been with us since they invented duplicating and has been popularised by photocopying; it's the copied form in one tone of clerical grey with your name typed in another shade. The Two-Tone is the bureaucratic fingers-up. Here's an example, a photocopy of a very old copy. Note the attention to detail:

Medical Research Council
in association with
Northwick Park Hospital
Management Committee

CLINICAL RESEARCH CENTRE

Watford Road, Harrow, Middlesex HA1 3UJ
telephone: 01-864 5311
telex: 923410

PERSONAL: 19.10.1981

Ref.No: 127/2/4561/56

Dear Mr.Shell
........Technician........................

    I regret to inform you that following your application in respect of the above post, you were not selected for interview.

I would like to thank you for your interest in applying.

Yours sincerely,

SHead

p.p. STAFFING OFFICER

This two-tone impersonality is probably the most curt and off-hand way of rejecting anyone. It also signals a dearth of creativity and is an indicator of the company's total lack of style; you wouldn't want to work for them anyway (well, maybe you would, but telling yourself so is pretty effective consolation).

45

The Word-Processed
Dispensing with simple duplication methods, some offices now rely on new technology. The word processor (a marriage of computer and typewriter) has taken over from the Roneo machine and reproduces stock rejection slips which look like personal letters.

You might *think* they're treating you as an individual, but they're expending even less effort. Press the right button, the machine prints your name on the rejection note held in its memory (it's called mail-merge) and here comes the 'personal' letter. All very efficient. Only the system isn't foolproof. All that technology, that devious expense, can go haywire — revealing that you're just another number on another long list of rejects.

But there's a triumphant feeling at having found them out. Like Mr. Godsi whose mail did not merge.

After applying to a well known oil and chemicals company (winners of the Queen's Award for Export Achievement) he waited patiently for the reply. A few months later it came in the form of a long, mechanically neat and supposedly 'personal' letter apologising for the delay, referring to the exceptionally high standard of applicant and regretting that Mr. Godsi would not, in this instance, be invited for interview. The writer ended his letter hoping the applicant would not be too disappointed by the difficult decision forced on the company. At this point the word processor, maybe affected by the pathos, gave up, spewing out a few garbled lines consisting mainly of I's, X's and Y's. The personnel manager signed the letter anyway, perhaps proving that machines can make it bad, but people only make it worse.

The Impersonal Insult
Part of the job of personnel officers is to care for personal feelings. It's ironic that so much of their time should be spent rejecting those for whom they should care. But while this is inevitable, it doesn't justify the *manner* in which they so often execute their distasteful task. Here's an example from an independent television company set up to investigate man's inhumanity to man. They bring a new low to rejection.

Date as postmark

To All Applicants,

Sometime ago you wrote to us about
the possibility of working on a
programme commissioned by Channel
Four. We are sorry to have been
so long in responding. The
resaon for the delay is simple -
nearly 2,500 people replied to
the various advertisements...
If you hear nothing by the end
of June, please assume that you
will not be contacted.

We are sorry that this has to be
an impersonal form letter, but
we do thank you for your interest
in us. Your letters were
tangible support for the conviction
that a need exists for the
programme we have been commissioned
to produce.

It might also be tangible support for the theory that a
lot of people want jobs.

The Poverty Trap

With more people chasing fewer jobs the pressure on personnel officers is becoming intense, leading to delays, cock-ups and a new form of administrative arrogance — ignoring the hopefuls.

It used to happen only to actors but now the hubristic 'don't call us, we'll call you' has invaded even the most conventional institutions. Applicants are being told, usually by circular, that if they haven't heard by a certain date, the job's gone. Listen to this particularly pathetic directive from a local council which blatantly admits to being too poor to be able to care.

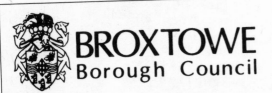

BROXTOWE
Borough Council

DIRECTORATE OF MANPOWER
BROADGATE HOUSE.
BEESTON.
NOTTINGHAM. NG9 2GH.

Tel: Nottm. (0602) 254871
Ext. 421 Ask for Miss Tomlinson
Our Ref. LMH/   A
Your Ref.
Date   24 May 1982

Dear Mr Turner,

Post: TRAINEE ACCOUNTANT

I acknowledge receipt of your application for the above post which is now under consideration.

Due to the ever rising costs of postage it is, unfortunately, no longer our practice to write to applicants again unless they are asked to attend for interview. If you hear nothing further it will mean that this vacancy has been filled.

I should, however, like to take this opportunity to thank you for the interest you have shown in seeking employment with this Authority.

Yours sincerely,

S Snowden
PP J W Silverwood
Senior Personnel Assistant

STYLE
They lack the panache to say it with love (let alone flowers) so they choose to communicate in probably the most anachronistic and clichéd language known. (Maybe their object is to bore those parts other business letters cannot reach).

The Tortuously Indirect
Instead of saying: 'Sorry, John, you haven't got the job', the writer has to come up with administratively meaningful phrases like:

- On this occasion you have not been successful
- We will not be pursuing your application any further
- We have to hereby inform you that your name has not been shortlisted for interview

On this occasion? Pursuing? Hereby?

Repetitive use of exhausted phrases is usually a ploy to make necessarily short letters unnecessarily long. Slavishly following the bureaucratic dictum of never using one word when you can get your secretary to type five, these scribes of doom never lie once when they can possibly do it twice.

The Double Lie
It's a common occurrence. Firstly, there's the 'we will be pleased to retain your application on file' fib which doesn't fool anybody. This lie usually follows the statement that the company has been overrun ('inundated' is also a favourite) by thousands of applications. Unless they're keeping them on micro-film, very few firms have the time, staff or space to store all the bumph.

The second falsehood runs something like this:

'We would, however, like to thank you for your interest in our organisation.'

Most people can't afford to be interested in the company — all they want is a job, anywhere and from anybody.

Never mind the message, feel the paper
If you're bored by the content of your letter you can spend many fascinating hours appreciating the extraordinary

creative effort spent by a few companies to produce a striking letterhead, while others appear to make a corresponding attempt to keep a low corporate profile.

A film company by the name of EARP attempts to reinforce its Wild West image by punching (bullet?) holes through its name and Thames TV reproduces a large frieze of London's Embankment on paper thick enough to make paper boats. In sharp contrast are the spendthrift borough councils, the BBC and worthy welfare groups who, it is hoped, use better paper in the lavatories than in their typewriters.

THE (SORRY) EXCUSES
You've heard of racialism. You've had it up to here with sexism. But did you know regionalism has returned, ageism plays its part and there's discrimination against short people?

Scared of a comeback, employers seldom give excuses, but occasionally their prejudices escape. Mr. Meredith did not appreciate one such slip.

Excuse 1 Regionalism
Aspiring architect Ian Meredith lived in Herefordshire, a major handicap it seems.

Dear Mr. Meredith, Thank you for sending us your CV ... We had a lot of applicants for our vacancy and felt it more sensible to see only those who lived in London first, and we have been able to fill the post ...

Ian was, of course, applying to London firms because he wanted to live in the capital.

Excuse 2 Dwarfism

National Provincial Bank Limited

ALL LETTERS
TO BE ADDRESSED TO
"THE MANAGER".

TELEPHONE Nº 26251/5.
TELEGRAMS: NATPROBAN."

Bristol, 1. 8th June 1951

7/BSS.
PRIVATE.

Mr. W. Chandler,
9 Sefton Park Road,
Bishopston,
BRISTOL.7.

Dear Sir,

We are extremely sorry to advise you that our Head Office have informed us that they are unable to proceed with your application for appointment to the Staff of the Bank as you are below the Bank's minimum height requirement of 5ft 4ins.

Yours faithfully,

[signature]

Manager's

P.S. We hope you will be successful in finding a position to your liking. *[initials]*

Mr. Chandler is now 5'7''. He does not work in a bank. — It appears architects, as Mr. Meredith discovered above, have to be prepared for prejudice.

Excuse 3 Ageism

The Architectural Press Ltd

The Architects' Journal

CB/CAB

Registered office 9 Queen Anne's Gate
London SW1H 9BY
Telephone 01-222 4333
Telex 8953505

Registered England 1175699

Paul Bird Esq
59 Hurst Park Avenue
Cambridge CB4 2AA

21 August 1981

Dear Mr Bird

Thank you for your letter of application. I think
I should tell you straight away that I am putting your
application low on our list. This is due only to the
fact that you, like me, are nearing permanent retirement.
The present holder of the post is aged 60 and I think it
would be healthier for the AJ to have a younger man in
the post who would possibly be closer to the new ideas coming
from emerging architects. It means replacing experience
with the brashness of youth, and if this becomes too
disastrous I will remember you!

Yours sincerely

Colin Boyne
Editorial Director

Excuse 4 Nationalism

David McClure discovered that being an expatriate can cause difficulties. He's lived in Britain all his life but holds American citizenship. He needed a job so applied to the BBC foreign service.

BRITISH BROADCASTING CORPORATION

PO BOX 76 BUSH HOUSE STRAND LONDON WC2B 4PH

TELEPHONE 01-240 3456   TELEX: 265781

TELEGRAMS AND CABLES: BROADBRIT LONDON TELEX

25th May 1982

Mr. D. McClure,
23 Cannon Place,
London N.W.3 1EH

Dear Mr. McClure,

Thank you for your letter expressing interest in the Trainee Writer post in this department. I wish that I could give you a more positive reply, as I was very impressed by your application and the evidence of your writing ability. But I am afraid that for various reasons I can only consider applications from British citizens in this particular instance.

It is a matter of great regret to me that it should be thus, as I am a frequent visitor to the United States and once spent a happy graduate year at Harvard, suffering no discrimination whatsoever - save perhaps from a Boston Irish traffic policeman who failed me in a driving test the first time round.

I hope you have better luck elsewhere.

Yours sincerely,

Leslie C. Stone,
Head of Central Current Affairs Talks

Cheering all Boston Irish traffic officers, Mr. McClure tried the logical alternative, the American Embassy.

EMBASSY OF THE
UNITED STATES OF AMERICA

Grosvenor Square
London W1A 1AE

May 25, 1982

Mr. David McClure
23 Cannon Place
London
NW3 1EH

Dear Mr. McClure:

Thank you for your letter of recent date in which you express interest in employment with the American Embassy.

We regret to inform you that Embassies abroad do not recruit American personnel locally, either in a permanent or temporary capacity. The American personnel at this and other Embassies are members of the Foreign Service and, as such, are recruited in Washington for assignment on a world-wide basis to meet the needs of our diplomatic and consular posts abroad. Vacancies, as they occur, are filled by transferring Foreign Service personnel from one post to another, or by assignment directly from Washington.

Should you, however, still wish to work for the U.S. Government overseas, it is suggested that you contact the Employment Division, Department of State, Washington DC 20520 for employment with the Foreign Service, and the Office of Personnel Management, Washington DC 20415 for employment with other U.S. Government agencies and departments.

Sincerely yours,

Kathryn J. Groot
Personnel Officer

In desperation he tried some NATO countries but discovered we're more united over the siting of nuclear deterrents than the location of jobs. With a sheaf of multi-lingual rejection slips Mr. McClure tried the only alternative — Channel Four. He got a job.

Excuse 5 Please forgive us, we're in a mess
Some excuses reveal little secrets about the state of the
employers' offices. Like this one from an Oscar winning
film company in Soho.

Dear Mr Newman,

I must apologise for the very long

delay in this reply to your letter.

It was in a file of letters to be

answered which inadvertently got

pushed under a pile of books --

this file has only just come to

light. I am sorry...

Excuse 6 Sorry we're bust

There's just no arguing with some excuses, as furniture designer Mike Smith discovered. After a couple of enthusiastic letters and awaiting his contract he received instead this letter from his prospective employer.

> Dear Mr Smith,
>
> As you may have heard, we are now in the hands of the receivers and this effectively puts the company into a very uncertain position. I regret, therefore, that we cannot pursue the filling of the designer vacancy...

For whom does one cry?

ENGO ENGINEERING

How to feel better
Lifting a rejected heart is difficult, but not impossible.
Here are a few suggestions:

1. With red pen poised examine the letter for mistakes in
   syntax, spelling and composition
2. Check the Tipp-Ex factor. Hold it to the light and read
   all the errors hidden behind the correction fluid. Mark
   with your pen
3. Think how you would re-phrase badly written sen-
   tences
4. Mark out of 10 and if it fails to attain 75% send it to
   someone writing a book on rejection

How to get your own back

1. Don't give up
2. Get a better job
3. And write a rejection letter to one or more of your more
   unimaginative prospective employers, like this serious
   one sent to a firm of accountants

Buckhurst Hill
Essex.
22 nd March 1980

Dear Miss Bradshaw,
            Thank you for your letter
of 12th march 1980.
   I have considered very carefully my portfolio
of job offers, and have decided not to accept
your offer.
   I would like to take this opportunity of thanking
you for considering my application.
            Yours Sincerely,

Showing Flair

In defence of hardworking, overburdened personnel officers it must be said that some do make that little extra effort, even using the Prime Minister's name to instil hope.

PO Box No 42 Hexagon House
Blackley Manchester M9 3DA England

Telephone 061-740 1460
Telex 667841/2
Telegrams Bridycor Manchester

Mr.A.D.Longstaff,
21, Maybury Close,
Frimley,
Camberley,
Surrey GU16 5HH.

ICI Imperial
Chemical
Industries
PLC

**Organics
Division**

makers of dyestuffs,
pigments and
industrial chemicals

Your ref	Our ref	Tel ext	Date
	MPP/TN		30th March, 1982

Dear Tony,

First of all, may I thank you once again for coming along for interview in Manchester last week. We found the two-day session both instructive and enjoyable and were most impressed by the quality of the young people that we saw.

As you may know the numbers in total that we are taking on are very limited and out of an original 600-700 applicants, we will only have interviewed approximately 30, of whom you were one. On this occasion I regret to inform you that we will not be asking you to join us, but can I please re-assure you that you left us with the clear impression that you would be an undoubted asset to British industry for the future and our task was very difficult in selecting the few from the final interviewees who we eventually selected.

May I personally take this opportunity of wishing you every success in your future career and express the view that I am sure you will find an interesting and acceptable position if you show the enthusiasm and intelligent approach that we perceived last week. Maybe the fact that Margaret Thatcher was once turned down for a job by ICI bodes well (or ill) for your future.

Best regards.

Yours sincerely,

M.P.Parker
P (Secretary)

C H A P T E R

WHEN YOU KNOW NO
MEANS NO

'"NO, THANK YOU" HAS LOST MANY A GOOD BUTTER-CAKE' (LANCASHIRE PROVERB)

Women are often (falsely) accused of saying no when they mean yes. Most writers of rejection letters try to make you think that they would *love* to say yes but are forced, by circumstances totally beyond their control, to say no. A minority don't conform at all. They want to say no, they mean no and they want you to be under no illusion about their negativity.

Take the case of James Butt, one of Britain's minor but respected composers who trained under Benjamin Britten and has a three inch listing in *Who's Who*. Hoping to impress his publishers with some sound commercial thinking he commissioned a market research report on his latest sonata. It predicted a potential world wide audience of 5,000,000 — a fair number for 1982 when war raged in the Falklands and the recession bit deep. Mr. Butt was confident as he slipped the score and report into his Suffolk post box. He shouldn't have been. Back like a bullet came the reply from Schott's, one of the world's largest music publishers. The writer was critical; so much so that he even found fault with Mr. Butt's lengthy address complaining that he would be pensioned off before he finished addressing the missive.

Besides comparing the sonata to torture, Schott's were extremely critical of Butt's estimated audience figure. Referring to Employment Secretary Norman Tebbit's 'get on your bike' statement, Schott's suggested that five million people might consider cycling to the Falklands instead of listening to the dramatic sonata.

Mr. Butt was not amused.

Brevity is seldom the forte of rejectors who eschew stock 'we regret' slips for the personal touch. Like Dickensian schoolmasters who kept personal canes, they feel it is their inalienable right to lash you with their negativity until you are so far down you'll never come up to bother them again. They're wrong. While experiencing catharsis with pen or typewriter they can inadvertently reveal things about themselves which can make you feel much better — ready to bounce back and fight on. The case of South African political refugee Tony Radley is a good example. Determined to find work in film production he wrote to every company in the book. He thought it wise to be quite open about his reasons for settling in

Britain and while most producers applauded his decision, one did not:

H—B HUGH BADDELEY PRODUCTIONS

PRODUCTIONS

Registered office

Vat Registration No.229 8144 46

64 MOFFATS LANE, BROOKMANS PARK, HATFIELD, HERTS. AL9 7RU   Telephone: POTTERS BAR 54046

18th December 1979

Dear

Thank you for your letter of the 11th December. I am afraid that we have no vacancies in this small and very compact production unit at the moment.

However, I think that I should be frank and say that if there had beem I would not be prepared to consider you for it. By a strange coincidence I have just returned from southern Africa where I have been producing a documentary film on one of the independent African states. I also spent a little time in South Africa itself.

I noticed how immensely the African state in which I worked was dependent upon the economy of South Africa, both for employment and for most of its food supplies and many other things. If South Africa ever falls through being rushed much too fast into control by inexperienced people the collapse and starvation throughout the southern part of the African continent will be so vast as to make Cambodia look like a Sunday school outing. And if the communists take control, as they probably would under these circums+ tances, all Africa would soon be under their domination. Pro- bably, with nowhere to refuel any plane or a ship between Europe and the East, most of the rest of the world would follow. Then concen- tration camps and replicas of Lubianca prison would spring up every- where and most of those with any ideas of freedom would soon find themselves incarcerated therein. I've made films in Russia too and know what I am talking about from personal experience.

I consider your desertion of your own country, the country that probably gave you a pretty good start in life, is despicable. I, like millions of my generation, fought against the tyranny of our time, Fascism. And somehow we smashed it, although at times it looked as though we would go under. The current enemy of freedom is called Communism and it, too, is marching forward, relentlessly and tirelessly. I suppose those of us who have given a little thought to het your generation are conducting yourselves shouldn't be surprised that there's not much fight in you, and in your case apparently, none. All I can say is that I hope you don't live to regret your lack of spirit.

If I were you I'd dash back to that efficient and attractive country and fight for it. Changes will come, and they will be much better for being evolved step by step, as they have been in many other countries. The wind of change is blowing in South Africa, but evolution is the only hope. Sudden change in that oart of the world, as things are at present, can only open the gates to the greatest tyranny of all -- plus starvation for hundreds of millions.

Yours sincerely,

Hugh Baddeley

61

A clear if not concise refusal. Tony rejected the advice but did not bother the producer again. Others more persistent than him have found that pestering the same person can have a positive effect, if only to improve the style, composition and content of the rejection letter. In some cases a postal relationship can develop — a sort of pen-friend-cum-pen-bully. Norman Lovett has such a relationship. He's an aspirant comic whose ambition is to write a successful situation comedy. He's bombarded the BBC with scripts for radio and television without making many people laugh. Some have made people quite cross. Once he mistakenly sent a TV script to the radio department and received a long missive from the clearly over-worked script editor.

Dear Mr Lovett,

I am returning this script to you unread, I'm afraid. I have just taken over the job of Script Editor, Light Entertainment (Radio). This is a radio post, and I am a radio producer. My desk teeters, and my brief case bulges with radio scripts, I haven't got time to read <u>them</u> all properly, let alone any television ones that get sent to me. I have to make some rules to prevent myself working all hours of the night outside office hours, reading jokes and going gradually barmy....

Mr. Lovett took the BBC's (Radio) advice and sent his scripts to their telelvision section, where he never became 'Our Norm' — but a relationship did develop.

Dear Mr Lovett,

I return "Sporting Myths and Legends" with many thanks for letting us see it...But I'm afraid that it's well below the required <u>extra</u>-high standard required by this form of comedy...It is also considerably shorter than the length we require, but the one consolation you might derive is that you <u>could</u> have written more and <u>still</u> have been rejected....

Back to the gag book went Norman. A few months later he produced a new script and had another letter from the same editor:

Dear Mr Lovett,

I'm returning "Four Good Seasons" as I'm afraid it really contains no potential whatsoever for us. The characters are unattractive and coarse, likewise their dialogue... You end with the stage direction "Generally Happy Scene". You must be joking. Many thanks for letting us see the script but in our opinion it's well below the standard of your previous rejections.

'You have to laugh at failure, it's part of a comedian's job,' says Norman. 'I can't remember how many scripts and tapes I've sent to the BBC. But I'm going to get in there one day. I'm sure of that.'

Most comics receive far shorter shrift. In 1961 Sidney Nesham sent a contribution to David Kossoff the actor/producer and teller of kindly Jewish stories. Back came the reply on a label stuck to Mr. Nesham's introductory letter:

Dear Sir

I return your script I would rather not make any comment. Except to say that most people send with MS. a stamp for its return.

DK.

Literary agents, who should perform an editorial sifting function to protect harrassed producers, sometimes fail in their task. They are seldom forgiven. John Lloyd, producer of *Not the Nine O'Clock News,* received a pile of very old jokes via an agent. It made him cross. He wrote back:

"This material is absolutely awful, totally unoriginal and completely unsuitable in every particular. I assume that either you have never watched 'Not the Nine O'Clock News' or you are mad. Whichever it is, please do something about it before sending me any more of this sort of tosh."

The prize for negative brevity must go to the Russians. When genealogist Noel Currer-Briggs discovered that his client's roots extended under the Iron Curtain he sent a letter to central records in Moscow respectfully requesting information on birth certificates. After the normal bureaucratic delay came the perfectly typed reply on official note paper: 'Nyet'.

Neil Sedaka was treated by the Russians to the same economy of words. As an accomplished classical pianist in the late '50s he was invited to demonstrate his talents in Moscow. Meanwhile his first pop hit *Oh Carol* was released which made Sedaka hot property in New York but did nothing for the cold war. Moscow withdrew the invitation, by telegram, in Russian.

It's not everyone who has the privilege of being brusque. BBC workers, for instance, are under strict orders not to abuse the public no matter how tiresome they can be. So producers have learnt how to be ultra-negative in a rather sophisticated twin-set and pearls way. Like this example of ragged-toothed Aunty biting back:

BRITISH BROADCASTING CORPORATION
LIME GROVE STUDIOS LONDON W12 7RJ
TELEPHONE 01-743 8000 TELEX: 265781
TELEGRAMS AND CABLES: TELECASTS LONDON TELEX

27th February 1976

Dear Mr. Foreman,

Thank you for your letter to John Gau.

I am sorry that we were not able to reflect your talents in "Nationwide on the Road" from Southend. I understand from our researcher that your broken-glass music was quite remarkable. Similarly, I am sorry that time ran out on us before we were able to capture the full range of your talking bird's vocabulary.

It is, of course, a matter for regret that you felt unfairly treated. However, I have to say that the production team did not quite share your own estimate of your skills as a musician and inventor, and the final decision on who and what should be included had to be left with them.

I am afraid it would be misleading to suggest that another opportunity to use you in a Nationwide programme is likely to arise in the forseeable future.

Yours sincerely,

(Stuart Wilkinson)
Deputy Editor
NATIONWIDE

Mr. L. Foreman,
82 Chalkwell Avenue,
Westcliff-on-Sea,
Essex.

Some rejectors, less skilled in the use of language, take a bizarre pleasure in their task and treat prospective clients rather too dismissively.

RECORDS
26 Alexander Street London W2 5NU
Telephones 01 229 7146, 1147, 01 727 9202
Telex 299694

REJECTED

Dear Hopeful

As must be pretty obvious by now, we haven't even got the decency to write a personal letter to you (but at least we've sent one).

If we've had it too long, we apologise; if it's not the right one, don't worry - it's probably better than the original one you sent in; and if there is no tape with this letter, then we've either lost it or are considering taking it further and putting it out as a hit under another name.

Thanks for sending it in anyway, and don't give up, even though the best record company has in fact turned you down.

This is an official rejection letter.

Yours

Eamon Bytback

Proprietor: Elcotgrange Ltd.
Director: D. Robinson
Registered Office: 11 South Square
Grays Inn London WC1 RSHE
Registered in England no.1289544
VAT no. 241 7112 01

If nothing else, these letters destroy Newton's Law that for every action there is an *equal* and opposite reaction.

CHAPTER

6

...BUT I HOPE WE'LL STILL BE
FRIENDS

'LOVE COMETH IN AT THE WINDOW
AND GOETH OUT AT THE DOOR.'
WILLIAM CAMDEN

Such are the problems of love's communications system that we quite often rely on the postal service to carry our messages; especially when we want to end it all. The same medium that carries our warm hearts is even more effective at transmitting our cold shoulders.

While personnel officers, editors and other professional rejectors aren't required to give excuses, lovers appear to be under Cupid's duress to explain why their hearts have stopped pounding. Their reactions are usually hopelessly inadequate. The one used most often is 'I need time to sort myself out.' (There are, of course, many banal variations.) Its broad stroke encompasses all perfectly valid reasons for ending an affair, like bad breath, frigidity and premature ejaculation.

> Dear Jeremy
> As you can see from the notepaper I'M staying at this Sweet little hotel in Scotland. The air here is lovely. I'M Sorry I did not say where I was going but as I Mentioned last Week I do feel that things have gone too far and I need time to sort myself out.... I don't know when I'll be back, but could you please feed Fluffy till I let you know what the alternative arrangements are...

Fluffy survived. The affair did not.

On the morning after a marriage proposal from a wealthy Londoner, a society beauty (who will have to remain nameless) was awoken by her future husband's chauffeur. He delivered a letter scribbled on a page of office foolscap.

Dearest Sue,

I'm really not behaving very well at the moment & I'm very worried that the more we see each other & the more we plan, the bigger will be the disaster at the end.

Post Pandora, I'm feeling very rough & need time to put myself together. I'm also very weak & find it easier to have a shoulder to cry on. Your beautiful shoulder to be more exact. The problem is that with you there are no half measures, and rightly so...

Love is precious, and you are a very loving person. At the moment, darling I'm not the man for you, I cannot find the will to sustain a loving relationship with you & give you in return what you deserve...

Darling, it is better that we don't meet for the time being. Please don't think too badly of me because I really don't want to hurt you & I know it will be much worse in a few months time. Don't think too harshly of me. Thank you, really, thank you, beautiful, wonderful person...

Notice how the writer conveniently glossed over the proposal of marriage by using the word 'plan' in the first paragraph. And towards the end his effusiveness increases in direct proportion to his galloping guilt.

Some excuses are more specific. What so often starts relationships also ends them. Sex.

Dear Michael,

I'm writing to say that I think

we shouldn't see each other again.

It is difficult saying this and

I'm not saying there's anything

wrong with you, but I just can't

keep on having it every time we

see each other, it's so inconvenient

in the car. Maybe when I leave

Donald it will become easier....

The Americans overcame this problem by making bigger cars and opening motels.

Bloomsbury writer Dora Carrington did not like sex at all. She threatened to end her affair with Mark Gertler if he didn't stop his carnal conversations. In this letter to him she sticks passages of his last letter on to hers — a literary-criticism-cum-lover's-rejection.

NEXT LETTER, WHEN YOU WRITE, WHENEVER YOU DO, DON'T MENTION OUR SEX TROUBLE ETC ETC ETC AT ALL, I AM HEARTILY SICK OF IT. JUST WRITE AND TELL ME ABOUT YOURSELF THE COUNTRY AS USUAL. AND IF EVER I WRITE ABOUT IT TO YOU, PLEASE TAKE NO NOTICE.

CUR FRIENDSHIP IS NO WORSE OR BETTER THAN ANY OTHER FRIENDSHIP. AT ANY RATE WE ARE INTERESTED IN EACH OTHER — ENOUGH. WHY SHOUD WE FUSS?

I WANT SIMPLY YOUR FRIENDSHIP AND COMPANY MORE THAN ANYTHING IN THE WORLD.

You wrote these last lines only a week ago, and now you tell me you were "hysterical and insincere". When you talked me about it at Gilbert's and   said you loved my friendship were you hysterical and insincere? Yes I know that your real love is "beautiful and not low". Do not think I ever doubted that.

Only I cannot love you as you want me to. You must know one could not do, what you ask, sexual intercourse , unless one does love a man's body. I have never felt any desire for that in my life: I wrote only four months ago and told you all this, you said you never wanted me to take any notice of you when you wrote again; if it was not that you just asked me to speak frankly and plainly I should not be writing. I do love you, but not in the way you want. Once you made love to me in your studio, you remember, many years ago now. One thing I can never forget, it made me inside feel ashamed, unclean. Can I help it? I wish to God I could.

Do not think I rejoice in being sexless, and am happy
over this. It gives me pain also.

    Whenever you feel you want my friendship and company
it will <u>always</u> be there. You know that. This is all I
can say.

REMEMBER THAT I WOULD SACRIFICE ALL FOR YOU, MY VERY LIFE
IF YOU ASKED IT OF ME.

You write this -- yet you cannot sacrifice something <u>less than</u>
<u>your life</u> for me. I do not ask it of you. But it would
make me happy if you could. Do not be angry with me for
having written as I have. And please do not write back.
There can be nothing more to say. Unless you can make this
one sacrifice for me. I will do everything I can to be worthy
of it.

Young love, presumably free from too much sexual activity, can generate other more complex problems, as this Rochester teenager discovered when the postman arrived to untie the love knot.

Dear Eileen,

I am writing to say that I don't want to go out with you anymore — I hope you don't mind too much, but it's the only thing I can do. I have enjoyed myself these past few weeks but at the moment don't want to go out with anyone for too long. Apart from that I've just had my haircut for health reasons, and do not intend to be-stir myself overmuch for about three months till I recover. I should have used the telephone but I've always been rather scared of the instrument so had to write.

Yours, Colyn

Not just one excuse but three here. The haircut seems the most reasonable.

As Fluffy discovered earlier, it's the plain practicalities of breaking up by post which cause the greatest problems. We appear to mark our lover's territory with loans of precious objects that are difficult to retrieve by letter, as this rejector discovered.

Dear Peter,

Thank you for the postcard, glad you had an amazing time. But you mentioned seeing each other again. Well, while you've been away I've been relieved from a lot of pressures and I really don't want those pressures and heavies back. Really, Peter, I'm not just being stupid. I don't hate you or anything like that, I just want to be left alone. Life has been just hell over the past month and I don't want to start resenting you or anything like that.

I don't think that seeing each other would be anything but destructive. I can't stop you from coming to the club, but I will ask you to please <u>not</u> come. Please don't ring or write to me either.

I just need time to get myself together. I don't know what to do about the pot plants. I guess you had better keep them 'coz it's going to be very awkwar getting them to me. I hope you take this letter serious because I sure as hell mean it to be deadly serious.

If she's prepared to lose custody of the pot plants, she *must* be serious.

Maybe the answer to love's problems is not to start the sweaty process at all. Groucho Marx, not known for his successes in love, was at least strong enough to deter the allure of Miss Dobkin. She invited him to New York for tea, but he knew it could lead to trouble. He replied:

Dear Miss Dobkin,

I wish I could accept your kind offer to tea and cookies but the whole project isn't feasible, logical or sensible. To begin with I am approximately 3,000 miles away and am tied up with my secretary. These ties are very strong. They are almost as sacred as the bonds of matrimony and because of this and many other reasons I am unable to accept your kind and generous offer. Besides, it is raining outside and I never go to New York when it is raining.

If you fail in most endeavours; you'll probably triumph in love. Unfortunately reality usually reverses this hopeful axiom; for successful people are seldom victorious in matters of the heart. Richard Burton married five times, Elizabeth Taylor seven times (twice to each other), Brigitte Bardot three times and Peter Sellers four. Think of all those complicated letters they had to write and receive.

And there are those achievers who discovered how quickly lovers can change from amorous acceptors into repelling rejectors. According to *The Book of Lists 3*, the following notables' marriages failed within a month.

1. **John Milton:** In 1642 the poet married sixteen-year-old Mary Powell who decided to visit her mother a month after wedlock. She didn't return.

2. Gloria Swanson: After three weeks of marriage to actor Wallace Beery the couple separated. She said she wanted a baby, he said he wanted a quiet life.

3. Katherine Mansfield: When the writer married musician George Bowden in 1909 she was already pregnant by another man. They spent one night together and she, overcome with guilt, left in the morning.

4. Rudolph Valentino: Hollywood's Great Lover proved that looks mean nothing. His wife, Jean Acker, locked him out of their honeymoon suite. Their marriage had lasted less than six hours.

5. Katharine Hepburn: She married socialite Ludlow Ogden Smith in 1928 and left him three weeks later.

6. Dennis Hopper: The actor/director married actress Michelle Phillips to prove that marriage and career were compatible. She left him after eight days.

7. Burt Lancaster: He married and left circus acrobat June Ernst within a few days.

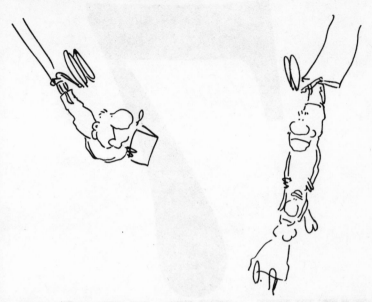

8. Germaine Greer: In 1968 the Australian feminist married *Cosmopolitan*'s first male nude pin-up, Paul de Feu. It lasted three weeks.

Which just goes to show that there's life after lost love.

7

THE EDITOR REGRETS...

'WE HAVE READ YOUR MANUSCRIPT WITH BOUNDLESS DELIGHT. IF WE WERE TO PUBLISH YOUR PAPER IT WOULD BE IMPOSSIBLE FOR US TO PUBLISH ANY WORK OF A LOWER STANDARD. AND AS IT IS UNTHINKABLE THAT, IN THE NEXT THOUSAND YEARS WE SHALL SEE ITS EQUAL, WE ARE, TO OUR REGRET, COMPELLED TO RETURN YOUR DIVINE COMPOSITION, AND BEG YOU A THOUSAND TIMES TO OVERLOOK OUR SHORT SIGHT AND TIMIDITY.'

CHINESE REJECTION SLIP

Every year 50,000 new books are published in Britain and about three times as many in the rest of the English speaking world: all preceded by millions of agonising decisions. No business knows such prolific rejection. And in no other sphere can the ability to be right be so heavily outweighed by the capacity to be wrong.

James Joyce's *Dubliners* was turned down by twenty-two publishers, Thor Heyerdahl's *Kon Tiki* by twenty, *Gone with the Wind* by thirty-eight and the authors of *The Peter Principle* approached sixteen unwilling companies before finding a taker.

James M. Cain had such a problem trying to persuade someone to take his novel that he changed its name to what for him had become a synonym of rejection. He noticed the doorbell always rang twice when his manuscript was returned. *The Postman Always Rings Twice* became a best seller.

After disagreements with his BBC bosses Frederick Forsyth resigned to work as a freelance reporter and writer. His first novel about an attempted assassination of de Gaulle didn't excite the first three publishers he sent it to; one said it had 'no reader interest'.

'The fourth [rejection] was telephonic, verbal and rather outraged because it was actually I who withdrew the manuscript after eight wordless weeks,' says Forsyth.

The Day of the Jackal, finally accepted by Hutchinsons, has sold over 12,000,000 copies worldwide and made Mr Forsyth a wealthy man.

Romantic novelist Catherine Cookson, dealing in matters kinder to the heart than assassination, has wooed the public with a succession of best sellers. But her start was disastrous. She sent one of her first efforts to a writing school offering free criticism. It was returned without covering letter but scrawled in red ink across the first page was:

Strongly advise author not to take up writing as a career.

'That would have put off the bravest heart. But looking back I realise now that that reader knew what he was talking about, for I had then to work a twenty year apprenticeship before I felt my efforts were suitable for publication,' she says.

Her next attempt was accepted by the first publisher who saw it. She's since made up for lost time and written fifty-five novels, the majority of which have been best sellers.

Richard Binns has only written four books, but then he's just started. And if he'd listened to publishers he might still be working as a computer consultant instead of making what can only be described as a very comfortable living producing his own books.

In 1980 he approached three companies with his comprehensive guide to France, called *French Leave*. One turned him down, another couldn't make up its mind and a third offered a contract so mean that he declined it. Determined to see his work in print he mortgaged his house, immersed his family in debt and published the guide himself. Against all predictions but his own, it went straight to the top of the best sellers list and stayed there long enough to recoup his expenses and much more.

'We didn't sleep at all that night we heard we'd topped the list', says his wife Anne. 'I kept hearing my husband laugh aloud every few minutes all night, as it suddenly hit him afresh.'

Richard Binns then published two best selling follow-ups and a limited edition guide, and he plans more. 'Doing it all myself has changed my life. Despite all the terrible financial gambles I've taken I've never enjoyed life this much,' he says.

Poet e. e. cummings also turned to self-publishing. Actually he turned to his mother who put up the money. He didn't forget his rejectors: the dedication in his first volume reads:

'No thanks to: Farrar & Rinehart, Simon & Schuster, Coward McCann, Limited Editions, Harcourt Brace, Random House, Equinox Press, Smith & Haas, Viking Press, Knopf, Dutton, Harper's, Scribners, Covici, Friede.'

The positive role mothers play in publishing should never be underestimated. In the '70s John Kennedy Poole wrote a funny novel about New Orleans called *A Confederacy of Dunces*. Publishers didn't appreciate the humour. So many turned it down that Mr. Poole killed himself. His mother refused to be depressed and fought on, finally succeeding with the Lousiana State University Press. It won the Pulitzer Prize for fiction in 1980.

At the turn of the century Beatrix Potter tried to persuade publishers to print her children's story book which she had also illustrated. *The Tale of Peter the Rabbit* was turned down by seven companies before she printed it herself. Miss Potter became rich.

So did former civil servant Richard Adams. Some seventy years later he wrote a different type of story about rabbits. *Watership Down*, an epic about bunny business in Berkshire, confused many publishers. Some thought it was no good, others were vaguely interested and they all agreed it was too long. One editor from Collins went to the trouble of writing Mr. Adams a three page letter complaining about the book's length.

He refused to shorten it and finally found a taker. It turned out that a lot of people, mainly adults, were interested in rabbits and the book quickly moved from cult interest to blockbuster sales; the volume in which romantic novelist Barbara Cartland is used to dealing.

She's written 350 books and with sales of 350 million has been named 'best selling author in the world' by the *Guinness Book of Records* (itself the subject of initial rejection). While never admitting to a rebuff in love, Miss Cartland has known it in publishing. She writes:

In 1960 when I was Vice President of the Romantic Novelists' Association, many of the young authors complained how difficult, if not impossible, it was to get their first manuscript published.

I thought I would test this by giving one of my manuscripts anonymously to a publisher and see the result.

At the time I had published 76 novels, besides a Book of Philosophy, 5 Historical Biographies, 9 Books on Sociology, 2 Autobiographies and a Biography of my brother, Ronald Cartland, who was the first Member of Parliament to be killed in the War. This book had a preface by Sir Winston Churchill.

I sent a manuscript under an assumed name to my agents asking them to make every possible effort to place it for a friend.

They gave it to a well-known publisher to Romantic Fiction who after a long delay returned it saying he could not consider publishing the book as it was, as it would not sell. He however advised the author 'to go on writing'.

I then sent the manuscript exactly as it was to Hutchinsons who published it in hardback in 1962 under my title 'The Wings of Love'.

It was followed by a paperback edition in 1967, another edition in 1970, was published in the United States of America

> and by now has been translated into
> almost every language in the world.
>   It is regrettably true to this day
> that young authors still have the same
> difficulty in getting their first book
> read, let alone accepted.

No one, it seems, is exempt from mistakes in judgement. T. S. Eliot wasn't. As editor at Faber & Faber he spent a large proportion of his time returning manuscripts, among them a few by George Orwell which he should have kept. Eliot could not be considered a great letter writer, but if his excuses were rather convoluted at least he showed little malice, as Stewart Deas discovered:

G.C Faber, Chairman C.W. Stewart R H.I de la Mare F.V. Morley & Morley Kennerley (u.s.a.) T.S. Eliot W.J.Craw

FABER AND FABER LTD PUBLISHER

FABBAF, WESTCENT, LONDON
MUSeum 9543 (4*lines*)   24 Russell Square London WC

26th January 1944.

Stewart Deas Esq.
6 Eldon Grove,
N.W.3.

Dear Mr. Deas,

        I am sorry for the delay in reporting on
City Chaconne.   I am rather in agreement with the reviewer
of your previous volume in the Times Literary Supplement,
that at first they appear to be rather formless notes but that
they do gradually appear to justify themselves and express
something collectively. I still feel, however, a certain lack
of metrical form in them.   I think they are worth publishing .
and I am sorry that I cannot ask Fabers to squeeze them into
our meagre list.

            With best wishes to yourself and your family,
                  Yours sincerely,

                        T. S. Eliot

How they say it
Publishers aren't the most creative people when it comes to saying no. Dealing in such volume they can hardly be expected to produce literary masterpieces of negativity every time around. Seldom do we have the pained pleasure of reading rejections of Samuel Johnson's quality:

'Your manuscript is both good and original; but the part that is good is not original and the part that is original is not good.'

Market Obsessions
Publishers' excuses (of which there are many) often show an obsessive fascination with a thing called 'the Market'. This adherence to monetarist apologia might be seen as a device to confuse and repulse creative contributors whose only experience with markets is their weekly purchase of fruit and veg.

'I'm afraid we will not be able to publish this material as we are reducing substantially our investment in this market. We also feel that there is considerable information going on to the market at present which covers the same ground.'

'I am sorry to disappoint you but I think it is best if I return your manuscript to you. I should emphasise that this is in no way a criticism of your manuscript, but merely a reflection of the state of the market.'

And if the market's vagaries don't quell the creative spirits, old favourites like 'can't squeeze it into the budget' or 'won't be able to persuade my colleagues to include it in our very full publishing programme' usually suffice.

It's always heartening to note that publishers find English as difficult as the rest of us. The double negative 'No, we are unable to . . .' is a favourite. Here's an example that includes most known excuses and cliches in one gloriously lumpy sentence:

'After careful consideration of your material w
decided that the market for this particular
content would be too small to be accepted for
inclusion in our future publishing programme.'

Blame it on the secretary.

The mould is sometimes broken, usually forced as was Gertrude Stein's editor, A. J. Fifield, through exasperation. In this instance it was Miss Stein's staccato and repetitive style.

Dear Miss Stein,

I am only one, only one. Only one being, one at the same time. Not two, not three only one. Only one life to live, only sixty minutes in one hour. Only one pair of eyes. Only one brain. Only one being Being only one, having only one life, I cannot read your manuscript three or four times. Not even one time. Only one look, only one look is enough. Hardly one copy would sell here. Hardly one. Hardly one.

Glazing the Glossies

Magazine feature editors are usually locked in despairing battle with contributors who besiege them with unsolicited articles. Sadly the two sides don't make much effort to understand each other. Editors claim to know their readers and what interests them. Contributors feel *they* know better, offering pieces that would enhance *Rotarian Monthly* but do nothing to excite readers in desperate search of pizazz.

Consequently editors have formed the unashamedly exclusive phrase 'not quite right for us'. *Punch* use variations on this theme often, sometimes twice in one paragraph.

'I think it's a perfectly presentable and useable piece, but not quite right for us. I am not sure that we can cope with quite so much sexual activity within the confines of one piece, and the style doesn't feel quite "us" (though, of course, it can be said that the fault lies with this magazine rather than yourself).'

The vast majority of hopefuls receive little printed slips. Their size is inversely proportional to their negativity. They're usually an extremely effective multilateral deterrent.

PUNCH OFFICE 23/27 TUDOR STREET LONDON EC4

The Editor presents his compliments, and regrets that he is unable to accept the enclosed contribution

Sorry we do not accept uncommisioned verse

But these slips are not always effective and some creativity breaks through only to meet the next hurdle, the critics.

'From the moment I picked your book up until I laid it down I was convulsed with laughter. Some day I intend reading it.'

Groucho Marx.

8

A REJECTOR'S RIGHT OF
REPLY

'REMEMBER
THAT IN GIVING ANY
REASON AT ALL FOR REFUSING,
YOU LAY SOME FOUNDATION
FOR A FUTURE REQUEST.'
SIR ARTHUR HELPS

It's Monday morning. They've got a hard day's rejecting piled up at the office. Their secretaries are finger-poised to type hundreds of 'we regrets'. They bounce up the stairs. Their step is light. And you know why? They're determined to be *nice*.

It appears that those whose job is rejecting others, are keen to be kind. This may come as some surprise to those of us who have received callous rebuffs from personnel officers, television producers, magazine editors and the people who should accept our inventions. But it seems their common characteristic is sensitivity. It's quite touching.

'The fear of hurting people's feelings is very strong. I'm probably more sensitive than most.'
John Lloyd, co-producer/director of
Not the Nine O'Clock News, now freelance

'It's horrible. I can't help feeling something about the pain I'm causing.'
Janet Richer, personnel officer

'I spend a lot of time on my rejection letters. I try to be gentle.'
Bob Haig, inventions scout

'Being in a position of power doesn't mean you're impervious to other people's feelings.'
Pamela Watkins, magazine features editor

Can it possibly be worse for them than for us? Is our quality sometimes lacking?

'If you really believe that someone is absolutely hopeless you have to be strong and honest, otherwise you'd be deluged by the fair proportion of nutters who regularly submit work,' says John Lloyd.

'I once received thirteen episodes of a situation comedy from a retired brewer with a heart condition (they often tell you things like 'I've only a short time to live and I wonder if you'd read this, my life's work'). Within a fortnight I had another thirteen. I started to panic.

'I dithered for another month and he sent me twenty-six more. This went on for some time and in the end I had a wheelbarrow of the stuff. I was paralysed by the problem. Eventually I sent it back with a nine page rejection letter and never heard another word.

'I went through two successful series without sending a stock rejection slip because they're so hateful to get. But in the end you just can't do it, you would go mad writing all those letters. And all the successful writers, or the ones who are about to become so and deserve to be read properly, wouldn't be read at all.

'I often quote the story of Douglas Adams, author of *The Hitch-hikers Guide to the Galaxy*. When I shared a house with him many years ago he was completely penniless. He couldn't get anything published and we had to buy him all his food and beer. Now he's happily living in tax exile.'

Advice:
Send only original work. Don't use emotional blackmail.

'As the recession lingers personnel managers are becoming more beleaguered,' says Janet Richer. 'Some people are now applying eighteen months before they've finished school or university. I don't know if *I'm* going to be around then, even if the *company's* going to be here. What can I say to them, but no.

'When rejecting my rule is that hopefuls receive letters of the same standard as their application. The bad ones get a stock slip.

'It's a pity people don't show much originality when applying. Sometimes they send a bit of torn foolscap with a scribble on it. Fifty per cent of the better letters use the word 'liaison' and very few spell it correctly.

'I've learnt never to lie. I don't say we'll keep their CV on file unless we do. It's far better to be honest and not raise hopes too high.

'All the letters we send out are advertisements for the company and I spend a lot of time seeing that there are no errors. But sometimes they slip through. And yes, sometimes I do make mistakes. I once rejected a now famous TV presenter because she got her well known husband to write in for her, instead of doing it herself.'

Advice:
Don't, as many do, send a photocopied or word processed letter. Show enthusiasm and don't be arrogant. Be persistent but not intolerable. If you want to liaise, spell it right.

'I only actively discourage people who have no original ideas,' says Bob Haig. 'For instance, every time *Towering Inferno* is shown on television we're flooded with new designs for fire escapes.

'We want solutions from the man in the street, he's the one who knows the problems. But it's a lousy way to generate new products.

'I have to be positive with every idea sent in. When I walk into the office I don't think 'Oh God I've got twenty-nine rejection letters to write.' Instead I hope that I'm going to find the thirtieth submission interesting, and make a big success out of it.

'When I turn things down I find that in most cases constructive criticism works and I consequently always use legitimate reasons. It pays dividends. After all, the inventor's next idea might be the big one for him and me.

'I used to word process most of the letters but then I realised that it was too harsh and much better to write personally.

'At the end of the day I sit down and read all my letters and think how I'd feel receiving one. If it's unnecessarily harsh I tear it up and start again.'

Advice:
Find out if it's been invented. If not, send the idea without spending too much on presentation. But don't, as many do, submit a messy doodle on the back of a cigarette pack. Listen to all criticism.

Contrary to public opinion Pamela Watkins's job can be laborious. Besides commissioning, checking and editing features, she also has to read the hundreds of unsolicited manuscripts that flow into her magazine. Subjects vary from the dangers of lead in petrol to increasing your bust size through positive thinking.

'I put all the unsolicited stuff in a drawer and tell myself I'll read it when there's a spare moment.

'It's usually awful or just not right for us. I type out the normal rejection note on a compliment slip. Sometimes I think 'Oh dear, that seems terribly cruel', so I stick the manuscript back in the pile again thinking that I'll write a decent letter when I have more time.

'I feel increasingly pressured as the stuff piles up. Sometimes I want to go out and stick it down a drain or leave it at the left luggage office.

'If I'm very late in sending a manuscript back I usually make some terrible excuse like "Due to staff changes I thought someone else had dealt with it", or "On moving my filing cabinet I discovered that your manuscript had fallen behind . . ."

'It's terrible saying no, no, no all day. When I leave the office I feel as though I've achieved nothing.

'But sometimes the boredom is broken by a truly appalling piece of writing. I once received a book — hundreds of pages — whose characters changed names half way through. Attached was a note saying: "For Fred, read John. For Joan read Jenny. For Mandy read . . ."

'And there was the short story where a man battles up a mountain to rescue a woman whose broken her leg in a skiing accident. They're alone on the mountain. The wind's blowing. She asks: "What's your name?" He says: "Let's not worry about names at a time like this, just call me Trevor".'

Advice:
Study the magazine carefully to see if your contribution will be suitable. Don't always write about yourself.

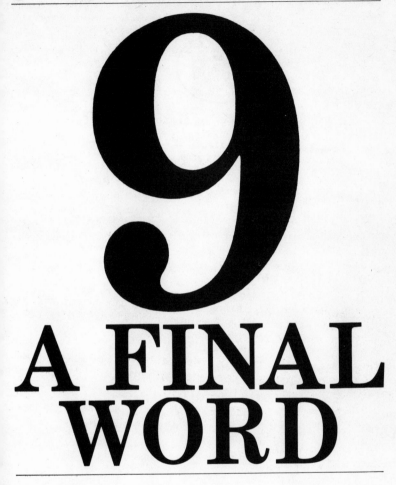

9

A FINAL WORD

'AT THE BEGINNING WAS THE WORD,
AT THE END JUST THE CLICHE.'
STANISLAW J. LEC

. . . from the Secretary of State for Employment, Mr. Norman Tebbit.

Caxton House Tothill Street London SW1H 9NF

Telephone Direct Line 01-213 6400

Switchboard 01-213 3000

Peter Knight Esq
6846 Fulham Road
LONDON   SW6 5SA

3/ January 1983

Dear Mr knight

The Secretary of State has asked me to thank you for your letter of 3 January, inviting him to offer a quote for your book.

On seeing your letter, Mr Tebbit's reacton was 'rejection letters are not often funny'.

Yours sincere,

D S HODGSON
Private Secretary

What's your reacton?